The Tiger Who Came to Tea

The Tiger Who Came to Tea

JUDITH KERR

PictureLions
An Imprint of HarperCollins*Publishers*

For Tacy and Matty

First published in Great Britain by William Collins Sons & Co Ltd in 1968
First published in Picture Lions in 1973
This edition published in 1998

19 20

ISBN: 0-00-664061-3

Printed and bound in Hong Kong

Once there was a little girl called Sophie,
and she was having tea with her mummy,
in the kitchen.
Suddenly there was a ring at the door.

Sophie's mummy said,
"I wonder who that can be.

It can't be the milkman
because he came this morning.

And it can't be the boy from the grocer because this isn't the day he comes.

And it can't be Daddy because he's got his key.

We'd better open the door and see."

Sophie opened
the door, and
there was a big,
furry,
stripy tiger.
The tiger said,
"Excuse me, but
I'm very hungry.
Do you think
I could have
tea with you?"
Sophie's mummy
said, "Of course,
come in."

So the tiger came into the kitchen and sat down at the table.

Sophie's mummy said, "Would you like a sandwich?"

But the tiger didn't take just one sandwich.

He took all the sandwiches on the plate

and swallowed them in one big mouthful. Owp!

And he still looked hungry,

so Sophie passed him the buns.

But again the tiger didn't eat just one bun.

He ate all the buns on the dish.

And then he ate all the biscuits

and all the cake,

until there was nothing

left to eat on the table.

So Sophie's mummy said,

"Would you like a drink?"

And the tiger drank

all the milk in the milk jug

and all the tea in the teapot.

And then he looked round the kitchen

to see what else he could find.

He ate all the supper
that was cooking in the saucepans . . .

. . . and all the food in the fridge,

. . . and all the packets and tins in the cupboard

. . . and he drank all the milk,

and all the orange juice,

and all Daddy's beer,

and all the water in the tap.

Then he said,
"Thank you for my nice tea.
I think I'd better go now."
And he went.

Sophie's mummy said, "I don't know what to do.
I've got nothing for Daddy's supper, the tiger has
eaten it all."

And Sophie found she couldn't have her bath because the tiger had drunk all the water in the tap.

Just then Sophie's daddy came home.

So Sophie and her mummy told him what had
happened, and how the tiger had eaten all the food
and drunk all the drink.

And Sophie's daddy said, "I know what we'll do.
I've got a very good idea. We'll put on our coats
and go to a café."

So they went out in the dark, and all the street
lamps were lit, and all the cars had their lights on,
and they walked down the road to a café.

And they had a lovely supper
with sausages and chips and ice cream.

In the morning
Sophie and her mummy
went shopping
and they bought
lots more things to eat.

And they also bought
a very big tin of
Tiger Food,
in case the tiger should
come to tea again.

But he never did.